Hi! I'm Darcy J. Doyle, Daring Detective,

but you can call me D. J. The only thing I like better than reading a good mystery is solving one. When I missed recess because someone took my homework paper, I had to do something about it. Let me tell you about The Case of the Choosey Cheater.

Other books in the Darcy J. Doyle, Daring Detective series:

Darcy J. Doyle
Daring Detective

The Case of the
Choosey Cheater

Linda Lee Maifair

ZondervanPublishingHouse
Grand Rapids, Michigan

A Division of HarperCollinsPublishers

The Case of the Choosey Cheater
Copyright © 1993 by Linda Lee Maifair

Requests for information should be addressed to:
Zondervan Publishing House
Grand Rapids, Michigan 49530

Library of Congress Cataloging-in-Publication Data

Maifair, Linda Lee.
The case of the choosey cheater / Linda Lee Maifair.
p. cm. — (Darcy J. Doyle, Daring Detective)
Summary: When a crime wave strikes the fifth grade, Darcy
Doyle tries to find out who is stealing homework papers.
ISBN 0-310-57901-5
[1. Schools—Fiction. 2. Mystery and detective stories.]
I. Title. II. Title: Case of the choosey cheater. III. Series:
Maifair, Linda Lee. Darcy J. Doyle, Daring Detective.
PZ7.M2776Cas 1993
[Fic]—dc20
92-39015
CIP
AC

Edited by Lori J. Walburg
Interior design by Rachel Hostetter
Illustrations by Tim Davis

Printed in the United States of America

95 96 97 / ❖ LP / 10 9 8 7 6 5 4

For my husband, with love.
Like Darcy's teacher, Miss Woodson,
he supports and encourages me
when I need it the most.
He takes my dream seriously
and believes in me,
even when I doubt myself.

CHAPTER 1

I'm Darcy J. Doyle. Some of my friends call me Darcy. Some just call me D.J. If I keep on solving important cases, pretty soon everyone will be calling me Darcy J. Doyle, Daring Detective. It's only a matter of time.

My last big case started when Mr. Ruiz asked us to turn in our math homework. Mine was missing.

I was sure I had put it inside my math book, next to the problems I'd done on page 48. I flipped the pages of the book a couple of times, thinking I might have put it in the wrong place. I didn't see it. I turned the book over, held it by the covers, and shook it. A gum wrapper and last week's menu fell out, but no math paper. I held it up over my head and shook it harder.

"What are you doing, Darcy?" Mr. Ruiz said. He was standing at my desk and peering down at me.

I could feel my face get hot. "Uh . . . looking for my homework, Mr. Ruiz."

He shook his head. "You know what it means if you don't have it."

I did. It was a school rule. If you forgot your homework, you had to stay in at recess and do it over.

Fractions aren't the sort of thing I like doing more than once, especially at recess. "But I didn't forget it, Mr. Ruiz," I told him. "I did it last night." Mom had even checked all my answers for me before prayers.

"And I put it in here this morning, Mr. Ruiz." I shook the book again. "I know I did."

"Rules are rules, Darcy." He walked back to the front of the room and called people up to do math problems on the blackboard.

I went through my math book, page by page. Nothing.

"Maybe you left it at home, on the table or something, D.J.," my friend Mandy suggested.

I shook my head. "Mom always checks to see if we've forgotten anything," I said. My brother, Allen, would forget to wear shoes and would never take his lunchbox if Mom didn't remind him.

Josh walked by on his way to the board to do a problem. He said, "Maybe you lost it on the bus."

I closed the book with a loud *whap*. "I don't ride a bus," I said.

"Maybe it fell out of the book on the way to school," Leon said.

I shook my head again. "I had the book in my

bookbag. And I emptied the bookbag in home-room this morning."

"Maybe she just didn't do it," Perry said. "Last time she didn't have it she said her dog ate it."

I gave him one of my looks. My dog, Max, *had* eaten it last time. He'd also eaten a gym sock and a candy bar I'd hidden under my bed. But I knew he hadn't eaten it this time.

I put up my hand. "I can't stay in at recess, Mr. Ruiz. We have a softball game. We're tied with the gold team. I'm supposed to catch. And my team will be one short if I don't play."

Mr. Ruiz didn't care. "You should have thought of that when you forgot to do your homework," he said.

An hour later I was sitting in the library, do-ing fractions, trying to ignore the shouts com-ing from the softball field. Terri was sitting on one side working on her social studies map and

Matt was sitting on the other writing his spelling words five times each. Neither one looked any happier than I was.

"What are you here for?" Matt asked when the librarian, Mr. Wilcox, wasn't looking.

"Forgetting my math," I whispered back. "I did it, but I couldn't find it when I got to class."

Mr. Wilcox looked up from the book he was reading. I did a couple of fractions. One-half plus three-fourths. One and one-third minus two-thirds.

Matt waited for Mr. Wilcox to go back to his reading. "That's funny, D.J. My spelling was gone, too. Disappeared right out of my bookbag."

"And I had my map all finished," Terri said.

"Three papers missing?" I said. "That's weird."

"It's a mystery!" Matt said softly.

12

Terri grinned. "Or a major crime wave at Bayside Elementary."

I looked up from my fractions and smiled. "Either way, it's a perfect case for Darcy J. Doyle, Daring Detective," I said, too loudly.

Sometimes daring detective work can be dangerous. Mr. Wilcox came over and told me he'd be seeing me tomorrow at recess, too.

CHAPTER 2

My brother, Allen, saw me putting my note-book into my bookbag. He groaned.

He was eating an orange, letting the juice run between his fingers and down his arm. I ignored him.

"What is it this time?" he said, wiping his hand on his clean T-shirt. "Somebody lose his lunch money?"

"It's a crime wave," I told him.

The only kind of waves he knew were at the beach. "A what?" he asked.

"Three kids had homework missing yesterday. Matt, Terri, and me."

"Maybe Max ate it again." Allen laughed. He wouldn't think it was so funny if Max ate *his* homework.

I gave him one of my looks. He started packing his own bookbag. "Who hired you?" he asked. "Matt?"

I shook my head. Matt hadn't exactly jumped at the chance when I'd offered him my services. "You gotta be kidding!" he'd said.

Allen was rooting through his lunch box to see what Mom had packed for him. He made a face at the bologna and cheese sandwich. "Then Terri did?" he asked.

Terri thought my new, regular two-dollar fee was way too expensive. She wouldn't even go for my super discount rate for fifth-grade girls—fifty cents. "Uh, no. Not exactly."

Every once in a while, when you least expect it, Allen's brain actually works. He laughed again, louder. "You hired yourself?"

What was so funny about that? This case was

important to me. I missed recess. My team lost the softball game. And I had to do my fractions twice. "Are you wearing those slippers to school?" I asked him. They were neon green and had comic book heroes all over them. I should have let him wear them. He was still laughing all the way to his bedroom.

I checked my homework twice. Once before I left for school and again when I unpacked my books in homeroom. It was all there. In fact, nobody had homework missing but Sammy Lee, and his wasn't really missing. He'd spilled a can of soda all over it and his mother had thrown it away. I was sort of disappointed that the crime wave was over already.

Then, on Wednesday, Mandy couldn't find her science words sheet. "I know I had it this morning, Mr. Ruiz," she said. "I looked up the last word in the library before school."

Mr. Ruiz wasn't any more helpful about science than he had been about math. And Miss

Woodson didn't take any excuses when Nick's essay turned up missing in language arts. The two of them were sitting in the library at recess while the rest of us watched Nick's team get creamed by the gold team.

I sat on the bleachers, my notebook in my lap, my pencil in my hand, not paying much attention to the game. "What's so interesting?" Miss Woodson asked me.

I told her about the big crime wave. "It's up to five now, Miss Woodson." I made a face at my notebook. "And it doesn't make any sense." I showed her my notes.

MONDAY: MATT — SPELLING. IN BOOKBAG.
TERRI — SOCIAL STUDIES. IN CLOSET. IN FOLDER.
DARCY — MATH. IN BOOK. ON DESK.

WEDNESDAY: MANDY — SCIENCE. IN NOTEBOOK. IN LIBRARY.
NICK — LANGUAGE ARTS. IN JACKET POCKET. IN CLOSET.

19

Miss Woodson made the same sort of face at the notebook that I had made. "Well . . ." She smiled. "I'm sure if anybody can figure it out, you can. You solved the Case of the Pampered Poodle, didn't you?"

"In fact . . ." She took her wallet out of her purse. "I'd like to hire you. Somebody's causing a lot of trouble. I'd like to get to the bottom of this crime wave. What do you charge?"

I couldn't wait to tell Allen. "Uh . . . two dollars?" I said.

Miss Woodson didn't gasp, scowl, or laugh the way most people did when I told them my fee. "Very reasonable," she said, handing me a dollar. "Half now, and half when the case is solved. Isn't that the way it's done?"

It was. I thanked her and slipped the dollar into the pocket of my jeans. I only hoped I wouldn't disappoint her. I pointed to my notes again. "Any ideas, Miss Woodson?" I asked her.

She laughed. "Oh, I'm not very good at solving puzzles. That's why I hired Darcy J. Doyle, Daring Detective."

I always did like Miss Woodson.

CHAPTER 3

The Homework Bandit didn't strike again until Friday. This time Andy Malone's fractions were missing even though he claimed he'd done them that morning. His name went on the "No Recess" list.

"But, Mr. Ruiz," Andy said, "I'm pitching today!" I knew exactly how he felt.

He didn't get any further with Mr. Ruiz than Mandy and I had. "You won't pitch from the library, Andrew," Mr. Ruiz told him.

Then, during language arts class, Cheryl Klein's tree poem was missing. She only got out of missing recess because she recited it, word for word, to prove she'd done it.

> Trees are green
> Trees are tall
> Their leaves are red and gold.
> They help us breathe
> And give us wood
> And live to a hundred years old.

I showed my notes to Miss Woodson again at recess during the softball game.

MONDAY: MATT — SPELLING. IN BOOKBAG.

TERRI — SOCIAL STUDIES. IN CLOSET. IN FOLDER.
DARCY — MATH. IN BOOK. ON DESK.

WEDNESDAY: MANDY — SCIENCE. IN NOTEBOOK.
IN LIBRARY.
NICK — LANGUAGE ARTS. IN JACKET POCKET.
IN CLOSET.

FRIDAY: ANDY — MATH. IN BOOK. IN DESK.
CHERYL — LANGUAGE ARTS. IN BOOKBAG. IN CLOSET.

"What do you think?" Miss Woodson asked me.

I didn't know what to think, but daring detectives don't like to admit that sort of thing to clients, especially clients who happen to be teachers who have already paid them a dollar. "Well, all the papers were taken out of books, or desks, or the closets," I said.

She nodded. "So it has to be somebody who has access to all those places."

I frowned. "That's the whole fifth grade . . . both classes, Miss Woodson." Our homeroom had math and science with Mr. Ruiz. His homeroom had language arts and social studies with Miss Woodson. Everybody "had access" to the books, desks, and closets in both places.

"Doesn't help much, does it?" Miss Woodson said.

I shook my head. "But there has to be a pattern here somewhere. I just haven't found it yet." I stared at the notes again, wishing the answer would jump right out at me. It didn't. "I wonder why—"

The cheers from the softball field drowned out my question. Perry Alexander and Theo Mitchell ran by me. "Gold! Gold! Gold!" They seemed real anxious to get back to their classes for a change. Poor Andy. Missing recess was bad enough without having a couple of guys brag about how they'd wiped out your team while you weren't there. I know; Perry and Theo had done the same thing to me.

"What I need," I told Mandy on the way home that afternoon, "is a motive."

She was softening up a wad of bubble gum, getting ready to try a couple of bubbles. "Mifff?"

When you're best friends with Mandy you learn to speak bubble gum. I nodded. "Motive.

You know, the reason the Homework Bandit is taking all these papers."

She blew a medium-sized bubble then drew it back into her mouth. "Dimmf da thermp?" she suggested.

I'd thought of that. I shook my head. "Somebody might not do his homework now and then, but nobody wouldn't do that much, that often. Or all those subjects at once. Besides, some of the papers were from Mr. Ruiz's class and some from ours. Our homework's not always the same."

The next bubble was bigger. "Not bad," I said.

Mandy smiled behind the bubble, drew it in, and softened the wad up again. "Maffeem thermp mamd?"

I thought about it, then shook my head again. "Who would be mad at so many of us?" I asked. I counted them off. "Matt. Terri. You. Nick.

Andy. Cheryl. And me." It looked pretty hopeless. Seven people had homework missing. Seven people who didn't have a whole lot in common.

Mandy huffed out a gigantic purple bubble.

"Mandy," I warned. She didn't listen. She was being what my dad called "overconfident." Huff. Huff. Huff. The bubble got bigger.

"Mandy, I think you're going a little too far with that . . ."

It took us a half hour to get the bubble gum out of her hair.

CHAPTER 4

"It was *this* big!" We were sitting in our favorite booth at the Bayside Family Restaurant, where we ate every Sunday after church. We'd finished discussing Pastor Jordan's sermon and were talking about my big case. I made a wide circle with the fingers of both hands to describe Mandy's bubble to Allen.

Dad glanced up from his Belgian waffles. He didn't seem very impressed by the size of Mandy's bubble, but his eyes did kind of sparkle when I described how it exploded. "Don't laugh with your mouth full of eggs, Allen!" he said. "It's rude."

Dad turned to me, and I tried to stifle a giggle. "Maybe your Homework Bandit will get over-confident, too," he suggested. "Maybe this whole crime wave will blow up in his face."

"Or hers," Mom put in.

"Couldn't be a girl." Allen sprinkled more pepper on his already black eggs. "Too smart."

Mom gave him one of her looks. "Not as smart as Darcy Doyle . . ." She looked at me. "Uh . . ."

"Daring, Mom," I said. "Darcy J. Doyle, Daring Detective." Why couldn't anybody remember it?

"Darcy J. Doyle, Daring Detective hasn't figured it out yet, has she?" Allen said.

Mom gave me a confident smile. "She will."

I hoped she was right. Right now, it didn't seem too likely. I wrote *overconfident?* in my notebook and stared at my notes. "The trouble is, there's no pattern, Mom." The detectives I read about in my mystery books were big on patterns. "The thief strikes one day, then not the next. He takes boys' papers and girls' papers. Some of us are in Mr. Ruiz's class; some are in Miss Woodson's."

I scowled at the list. "If I was going to take homework papers, I sure wouldn't take Nick's language arts . . . or my fractions. He's about as good at writing essays as I am at adding three-fourths and two-thirds."

Dad wiped a dab of whipped cream off his upper lip with his napkin. I would have just licked it off myself, but Dad's as big on good table manners as daring detectives are on patterns.

"There has to be some reason he took those papers, Darcy," he said. "You find that reason, and you might get somewhere."

It made sense. I added *reason for those papers?* to my notes and thought about it over a couple

bites of pancakes. Why us? Two of us were in the band. Three were on the newspaper staff. And Andy, Nick, and I had all missed . . .

"Whoopie!" I yelled.

Everybody turned to stare at me. Mom's mouth fell open. Dad's face turned pale. Allen even stopped stuffing himself with hash browns.

I felt my face get hot. "Uh . . . I found the connection, Dad. You know . . . the motive, Mom?" I waited for a lecture about working on a case and reading at the table and shouting "Whoopie" in the Bayside Family Restaurant.

"Pass me the sugar, will you, John?" Mom asked.

"Certainly, dear," he said.

CHAPTER 5

I told Nick and Andy my idea out on the playground before school on Monday morning. They didn't exactly congratulate me on my great detective work.

"You're all wet, Darcy!" Andy told me.

Nick nodded in agreement. "What makes you think it's somebody on the gold team anyway?" he said.

"The homework thief only strikes on Monday, Wednesday, and Friday, right?" I smiled proudly, but they didn't get it. "You know, the days we play softball."

"What about Mandy and Matt?" Nick asked. "They had homework taken and their teams weren't playing the gold team those days."

"And what about Cheryl and Terri?" Andy added. "They don't play softball at all."

I had that figured out, I was sure of it. "Diversions," I said. I smiled proudly again. They didn't get it this time either. "You know, diversions?" I said. "Phoney clues? False trails? A few extra victims to throw us off. That's why there wasn't any pattern."

"Pattern?" Andy said, as if I were speaking Chinese.

I glanced at my watch and sighed. There wasn't much time before the last bell. I explained the whole thing to them again. How every day that we played softball, somebody had homework taken. And every time homework was taken, somebody who was going to play the gold team didn't get to play. And every time one of those key players stayed in for recess, the gold team won.

"The thief wasn't interested in the homework at all, just the kids who did it," I said. "We didn't have a homework bandit. We had a very choosey cheater!"

"I don't know, Darcy," Nick told me. "Some of the homework was taken in Mr. Ruiz's room and some in Miss Woodson's. Nobody on the gold team could have gotten to all those papers."

He had a point. I thought it over as we made our way through the front door and down the hall past the office. "Maybe we're not looking for one choosey cheater," I said. "Maybe we're looking for a couple of them." That would explain how so many papers turned up missing in both places.

Nick still didn't buy it. "Maybe it's a whole gang," he said. "Like Jesse James?" We'd been studying the Old West in social studies.

"Yeah," Andy said, poking Nick in the ribs as if it was the best joke he'd heard in years. "Maybe everybody on the gold team is a home-work bandit!"

I would have given them one of my looks, but they'd turned down the hall toward Mr. Ruiz's homeroom, laughing all the way.

I followed Mandy into Miss Woodson's room and back to the coat closet. "Do you think I'm all wet?"

She pretended to be taking books out of her bookbag. "Well . . ." she said, talking more to the books than to me, "I think it might be a good idea if you had a little proof before you told Miss Woodson this idea of yours."

I hung my bookbag on the hook next to hers. I was annoyed. I was right; I knew it. "It's Mon-day and my team plays the gold team today," I said. "We'll see who's all wet when somebody

from my team ends up with missing homework and we lose the game!"

A few hours later I was shaking hands with the kids on the gold team. "Good game," we told one another as we filed by.

Perry Alexander squeezed my hand, hard. "You look real disappointed about something, Darcy." He grinned at me.

Theo Mitchell didn't even shake my hand. He just smiled, a smug, mean little smile.

It was almost as bad as the last time we'd played them and they'd gloated about my missing the game. The worst of it was that I *was* disappointed. It was Monday, but nobody had any homework missing. None of my teammates had to stay in at recess. We even won 8 to 7. Instead of being happy, I was worried. Maybe Darcy J. Doyle, Daring Detective, was all wet after all.

CHAPTER 6

"I'm giving up the detective business," I announced after grace that night at dinner.

I thought my parents would be relieved. Sometimes my Daring Detective work made life what Mom called "interesting." And Dad was always telling me not to go snooping around, bothering people. But neither one of them smiled.

"Case not going well?" Dad said, passing me the mashed potatoes.

I put a glob of potatoes on my plate, passed the bowl to Allen, and shook my head. I told him about my idea and how it had all fallen apart. "Andy says I'm all wet."

Allen looked up from the mountain of mashed potatoes he was building on his plate. He laughed. "That's what Billy Blackburn said."

I put down my fork. "When did Billy Blackburn say I was all wet?"

Allen was spooning a river of gravy into the gully he'd made in his mountain. "This morning. On the way to school."

I couldn't believe it. "You told Billy Blackburn that I thought the homework bandit was somebody on the gold team?"

By that time, he had a mouth full of potatoes and gravy. "Smmrf. Wymm nuft?"

"Allen Ryan Doyle!" Dad said before I had the chance to. At first I thought he was going to give him a lecture on talking with his mouth full. "Didn't you know that what Darcy told us yesterday at breakfast was confidential?"

Allen swallowed his mashed potatoes. "Confi . . . what?" he said.

"Confidential!" I told him. "You weren't supposed to blab it to everybody!"

He looked insulted. "I didn't blab it to everybody," he said. "Just Billy Blackburn and Dwayne Mitchell. They said you'd never figure it out and I said you already did and that's when I told them . . ."

"Dwayne Mitchell!" I wondered how upset Dad would get if I dumped my mashed potatoes on Allen's head. "Dwayne Mitchell whose brother Theo is on the gold team?"

He nodded as if he couldn't see what the fuss was all about. "Yeah, why?"

I decided the mashed potatoes wouldn't be a good idea. I attacked my meat with my fork and just glared at my brother. "No wonder nobody's homework was missing today. The thief knew ahead of time that I'd be expecting it."

"But I thought you'd want me to show them . . ." Allen looked from me to Dad to Mom. Nobody looked too pleased with him. He began to eat very quickly.

I dug into my roast beef. Finding out you're not all wet is good for the appetite. "May I take my dessert to my bedroom, Mom? I've got homework to finish, and I want to work on my case," I said.

Dad took a muffin out of the bread basket. "I thought you were getting out of the detective business." He tried not to smile.

"I can't quit now, Dad," I told him. "You know what Pastor Jordan said about using your talents. Besides, Darcy J. Doyle, Daring Detective, is about to crack this case wide open."

Allen spread his peas around on his plate so that Mom would think he'd eaten most of them.

"How do you plan to do that?" he asked.

I had no idea. "I can't tell you, Allen Doyle," I said. "You'd probably announce it over the loudspeaker tomorrow morning."

He stuck his tongue out at me. With a mouth full of roast beef and mashed potatoes, it looked pretty disgusting, but I didn't mind too much. Dad sent him to his room without any dessert.

CHAPTER 7

I sprawled out on my bedroom floor, my spelling workbook on one side, my daring detective notebook on the other, and my slice of chocolate cake on a paper plate in the middle.

I took a big bite of the cake. It was delicious. Max came in and sat down beside me, drooling over my shoulder. He whined and gave me his paw. Good old Max. Always volunteering to help with a tough case.

I gave him a bite of cake, letting him lick the icing off my fingers. Then I picked up my spelling book. *Persistent.* I wrote my sentence on a piece of paper. *Darcy J. Doyle, Daring Detective, is very persistent.*

I put down the spelling book, shared another bite of cake with Max, and picked up my notebook. Max whined again. I read him my list of suspects. "Perry. Theo. Latonya. Debbie. Jason. Brett. Emily. Danny. Enrico. And Jon."

It was a long list. Everybody on the gold team. I helped myself to another bite of cake. Max whined again. "I know," I agreed. "We need a way to narrow it down, but it won't be easy." Good old Max is very sympathetic. He gave me his paw.

I shared the bite of cake and went back to my spelling lesson. *Annoying. Brothers can be very annoying,* I wrote.

I put down the spelling list and picked up my notebook, frowning both at the chocolate smudges and at the long list of suspects on the page. I had to go about this in what Mr. Ruiz would call "the scientific method." Who could I cross off the list?

I shoved Max's nose away from my cake plate. "In a minute," I told him. I crossed Danny and Emily off the list. They'd been absent last week, Danny on Wednesday and Emily on Friday. "And Enrico comes in on the transfer bus," I told Max. "The papers would have been gone before he got there." I crossed his name off the list too.

I finished the cake, leaving a bite, a few crumbs, and some smeared-on icing for Max to finish. "Not bad," I told him. "I—"

"Darcy!" Mom called from down the hall. "Mandy's here." I'd forgotten she was coming over to study for tomorrow's social studies quiz. I went down to the living room to meet her. As we walked back to my room, I told her all about how Allen had blabbed my idea to Theo Mitchell's brother.

"Then you were right!" she said.

I paused with my hand on my doorknob and nodded. "It was somebody on the gold team."

"Who?" she asked.

I had my suspicions but no real proof. "I'm not sure," I told her. "Max and I were just narrowing down the list of suspects when you came."

"Max was helping you?" Mandy grinned, as if she thought I might be joking.

"Sure," I said. "I couldn't solve a case without the help of my faithful bloodhound, Max."

Mandy followed me into my room. Her eyes got big and she looked as if she was trying hard not to laugh. "Yeah," she said. "I can see what a help he is."

What was left of the paper plate and my homework lay in shreds at his feet. He held up his paw and dropped a piece of soggy, mangled notebook paper on the floor in front of him.

Mandy had her hand over her mouth, holding in the giggles.

I walked over and picked up the wad of paper and smoothed it out. It was the list of suspects from my notebook. Perry. Theo. Latonya. Debbie. The rest of the list was gone. Mandy nearly choked on her giggles.

I gave her one of my looks. "Didn't I tell you?" I held out what was left of the paper for her to see. "My faithful bloodhound helps me on all my cases. Good old Max has narrowed the list down for me already."

CHAPTER 8

"I want you to put all your homework papers in this box," Miss Woodson announced on Tuesday morning.

"All of them?" Sammy asked. "Social studies and language arts together?"

Miss Woodson nodded. "We'll sort them out as we need them." She handed the box to Sammy, who put his papers inside, then passed the box back to Tiffany Farrel. A few minutes later the box was back up front with Miss Woodson again.

"I'll just keep this on my desk," she said. "For safekeeping." Mr. Ruiz did the same thing when we went to his room for science and math. It worked. Nobody missed recess.

I wasn't surprised to see Perry Alexander and Theo Mitchell huddled together in the far corner of the playground over by the tool shed. I dribbled a basketball over in their direction. "Who's pitching in the big game tomorrow?" I asked. The gold team was playing my team, the blue team, for the softball championship.

They were always arguing about it. "I am," Perry and Theo said at the same time.

"At least you're lucky enough to have two pitchers," I said, as if I really envied them. "If one of you can't play for some reason, the other one gets to pitch. If Josh, our pitcher, doesn't play, we're in real trouble."

Perry and Theo smiled at one another. "Isn't that too bad?" Theo asked.

"Yeah, real pitiful," Perry agreed.

I dribbled away.

The next day we put our papers in the boxes at the front of the room as we came in the door. Miss Woodson kept a sharp eye on them until we switched classes for math. We came back for language arts before lunch. Miss Woodson asked me to pass out the homework papers so we could check our subjects and verbs.

I called the names and people came up front to get their papers. "Nick. Sammy. Josh."

Perry Alexander's mouth dropped open.

"That's all," I told Miss Woodson. I set the box back on her desk.

Perry Alexander's mouth opened further.

"Number one," Miss Woodson said. "Josh?"

Perry Alexander's lower jaw just about touched his desk.

"*Horses* is the subject. *Were running* is the verb," Josh read from his paper.

"Number two? Mandy." Miss Woodson got up from her stool and walked back to where

Perry Alexander was frantically looking through his English book. "Is there something wrong, Perry?"

"I didn't get my paper back, Miss Woodson," Perry told her. "I thought maybe . . ."

Miss Woodson looked surprised. "I didn't think you'd forget your paper today, Perry. I thought you wanted to pitch in the big game."

Perry's face turned red. "I didn't forget it, Miss Woodson! I'm sure I put it in the box this morning. I *am* going to pitch today." He and Theo had had another big argument about it that morning before school.

Miss Woodson shook her head. "Oh, I'm afraid not, Perry. You know the rules. No homework, no afternoon recess." She turned around as if the matter was settled. "Number two, Mandy," she repeated.

"*Puppies* is the subject and—"

"But Miss Woodson!" Perry interrupted. "My

paper was there. My mother helped me with it this morning. Somebody must have taken it from the box."

"Why would anybody want to do that?" she asked him.

"So I couldn't play." His face went pale, as if he'd just had a sudden, terrible idea. "Somebody who didn't want me to pitch," he said.

Miss Woodson didn't have much sympathy. "Everybody else had to stay in when their papers were missing, Perry," she said. "It wouldn't be fair to let you play. Theo will have to pitch today."

Perry slumped down in his desk. By the time the lunch bell rang he looked like he was ready to spit nails. I didn't feel very sorry for him.

I waited until the other kids had left the room and there was nobody left out in the hall.

"You're pretty good at acting, Miss Woodson," I told her.

She smiled. "So are you and Josh," she said. "I almost believed myself that his worksheet was still there and he was reading the answers from that blank sheet of paper you gave him."

She put her hand on my shoulder as we walked toward the door. "You're also a pretty good detective," she said.

CHAPTER 9

I peered around the corner of the tool shed. Sure enough, Perry Alexander was dragging Theo Mitchell across the playground—right in my direction. Quickly I ducked back. Their voices grew louder.

"Will you let go of me!" Theo told Perry. "You're going to sprain my pitching arm!"

"I should wring your neck!" Perry told him. He let go of Theo and put his hands on his hips. "Very clever, Theo."

Theo looked as if he didn't have the slightest idea what Perry was talking about. "What—"

"You were supposed to take Josh's paper, remember?"

Theo looked more confused than before. "I did. When Miss Woodson was handing back our essays."

"Sure you did." Perry shoved Theo back toward the shed. "That's why I'm missing recess . . . and the chance to pitch in the game."

Theo's face got red. "Wait a minute. Are you accusing me of—"

"You rat," Perry told him. "We work together on this homework bandit thing for a week and then you take my paper so you can pitch in my place." He took a swing at Theo.

Luckily, Theo ducked. "I didn't take your paper, Perry. Honest. I took Josh's. I threw it in the trash in the lunch room . . . just like the others. In the blue can. Go look for yourself."

"I think I will!" I stepped out from behind the tool shed.

Perry and Theo glanced at one another then

back to me. They didn't look all that happy to see me.

"You can't prove a thing," Perry said.

"Sure I can. All I have to do is go to the lunch room and get Josh's paper out of the blue trash can. Josh's paper with Theo's fingerprints all over it," I added, for effect. "They don't empty the trash until the third and fourth grade finish eating."

"Josh's paper?" It was Perry's turn to look confused. "Josh had his paper in class this morning."

"I'm afraid not, Perry." Miss Woodson came out from behind the shed where she'd been listening to the whole conversation.

Perry and Theo looked like they were going to faint.

I smiled. "Your paper was there, Perry. Josh's was missing."

"What?" Perry's face turned red again, and

for a minute I thought I might have to duck. "You mean it was all a . . . a joke?"

"No," I said. "It was a daring detective trap."

Perry and Theo argued about whose idea the whole thing was and who was the dumbest all the way to the principal's office. Neither of them was there when the blue team beat the gold team 10 to 5 that afternoon.

"Good work, Darcy," Miss Woodson told me after the game. She didn't mean just my catching either. She handed me a dollar bill, the other half of my fee.

I used part of it to buy a pack of chocolate cupcakes . . . one for me and one for Max. The rest of it I put in the jar I use to save money for my mystery books. All except for one shiny new penny I'd gotten back in change from the cupcakes. I taped that into my notebook of Important Cases Solved by Darcy J. Doyle, Daring Detective.